DATE DUE

DAN QUISENBERRY

FRANK WHITE

MIKE SWEENEY

LOU PINIELLA

BO JACKSON

HAL McRAE

JEFF MONTGOMERY

CARLOS BELTRAN

AMOS OTIS

WILLIE WILSON

GEORGE BRETT

BRET SABERHAGEN

KC
NIKE

THE HISTORY OF THE KANSAS CITY ROYALS

WAYNE STEWART

CREATIVE EDUCATION

Published by Creative Education, 123 South Broad Street, Mankato, MN 56001

Creative Education is an imprint of The Creative Company.

Designed by Rita Marshall.

Photographs by AllSport (Peter Brouillet, Jeff Gross, Donald Miralle, Doug Pensinger, Earl Richardson), Icon Sports Media (David Seelig, Chuck Solomon), Anthony Neste, Sports Gallery (Al Messerschmidt), SportsChrome (Michael Zito)

Library of Congress Cataloging-in-Publication Data

Stewart, Wayne, 1951- The history of the Kansas City Royals / by Wayne Stewart.

p. cm. — (Baseball) ISBN 1-58341-211-5

Summary: Highlights the key personalities and memorable games in the history of the team, begun in 1969, whose wealthy owner, Ewing Kauffman, vowed to make the Royals into champions.

1. Kansas City Royals (Baseball team)—History—Juvenile literature. [1. Kansas City Royals (Baseball team)—History. 2. Baseball—History.] I. Title. II. Baseball (Mankato, Minn.).

GV875.K3 S74 2002 796.357'64'0977841l—dc21 2001047881

First Edition 9 8 7 6 5 4 3 2 1

HALFWAY

BETWEEN AMERICA'S EAST AND WEST COASTS SITS Kansas City, Missouri. This city of nearly half a million people is known as a major educational center that boasts more than a dozen colleges and universities. Kansas City is also known as a great sports town, and fans of the city's professional football team—the Chiefs—are renowned for their loyalty and enthusiasm.

Another professional franchise that makes its home in Kansas City is a baseball team called the Royals, which joined the American League (AL) as an expansion team in 1969. Missouri had briefly been home to another big-league team called the Kansas City Athletics, but that club moved to the West Coast in 1968 to become the Oakland Athletics. Known for their hardworking,

LOU PINIELLA

scrappy style of play, the Royals quickly earned a devoted fan following in the heartland.

In one **1969** game, infielder Bob Oliver rapped six hits in six at-bats, including two homers.

{A SLOW RISE} In their first season, the Royals managed to win 69 games, an impressive total for an expansion club. Perhaps the team's best player was 25-year-old Lou Piniella. The outfielder led the team in hitting that year, and in his next four seasons with Kansas City, he batted above the .300 mark twice. Piniella was known for his intelligence and toughness, qualities that would make him a successful big-league manager after his playing days came to an end.

Bob Oliver, who spent time at first base, third base, and the outfield, was another key player. He provided some much-needed offensive punch for the young team, clouting 27 home runs and driving in 99 runs in 1970. In 1971, Piniella, Oliver, and pitcher

JEFF MONTGOMERY

Fleet-footed outfielder Amos Otis represented Kansas City in five All-Star Games.

AMOS OTIS

Dick Drago continued to shine as the Royals rose to second place in the AL Western Division.

Kansas City's pitching in those early days also revolved around Ted Abernathy and Steve Busby. Abernathy slung the ball toward the plate with a unique sidearm throwing style. In 1971, he racked up 23 saves, and a year later, he posted a stunning 1.71 ERA. Busby might have become an all-time great had a shoulder injury not cut his career short. From 1973 to 1975, he averaged nearly 19 wins per season and is still the only big-league pitcher ever to toss a no-hitter in each of his first two seasons.

John Mayberry became the first Royals player to drive in at least 100 runs in a season (in **1972**).

While Abernathy and Busby led the Royals on the mound, veteran second baseman Cookie Rojas and speedy outfielder Amos Otis picked up much of the offensive load. Otis roamed center field for 14 years for the Royals and electrified fans with his base-stealing

JOHN MAYBERRY

KC

Today's Royals are gunning for the third AL pennant in the club's history.

JOE RANDA

prowess, collecting a league-leading 52 steals in 1971. These players helped the Royals finish in second place in the AL West in 1973 and 1975. And Kansas City was just getting started.

In **1977**, Jim Colborn threw the third no-hitter in club history (Steve Busby threw the others).

{THE GREAT LATE '70S} The Royals won AL West crowns in 1976, 1977, and 1978. Their success was due in large part to a superb defense headed by new second baseman Frank White and shortstop Fred Patek, who formed an acrobatic double play duo. The agile White was perhaps the game's best defensive second baseman, while Patek was a 5-foot-4 speedster who led the AL in stolen bases in 1977. Patek was once asked how it felt to be the smallest player in the majors. "A heck of a lot better than being the smallest player in the minors," he replied.

Even though each of the Royals' three division-winning seasons ended with a playoff loss to the New York Yankees, fans

FRANK WHITE

came out in droves to watch the hustling Royals. Some of the players for whom fans cheered loudest were pitchers Dennis Leonard and Paul Splittorff and first baseman John Mayberry.

Leonard averaged 19 wins a year from 1976 to 1978, and Mayberry emerged as the franchise's first true slugger. In his first six seasons with the team, he slammed an average of 24 home runs a year.

And then there was George Brett, considered by many to be the greatest Royals player ever. The burly third baseman broke into the majors with Kansas City in 1973 and quickly became a star. In 1976, the future Hall-of-Famer led the AL in batting average, hits, and triples, lashing one line drive after another into the outfield.

George Brett was an aggressive runner, leading the AL in triples in **1975**, **1976**, and **1979**.

Over the course of his career, Brett played in 13 All-Star Games and became the Royals' all-time leader in every offensive category except stolen bases. He also established himself as one of the toughest outs in baseball. "George throws a little fear into you," said Atlanta Braves manager Bobby Cox. "All you can do with him is hope he hits the ball at somebody and it isn't hard enough that it knocks your guy over."

{A ROYAL PENNANT} In 1980, the Royals went 97–65 to again win their division. They then finally won their first AL

GEORGE BRETT

KC

pennant, capturing the flag when Brett blasted a dramatic, upper-deck home run in game three of the AL Championship Series (ALCS) against the Yankees. Kansas City fans were jubilant, sure

that it was their year at last. Unfortunately, the Royals could not take the final step, falling to the Philadelphia Phillies in the World Series.

During that season, Brett—who was named the AL Most Valuable Player (MVP)—almost reached the .400 plateau, finishing with a .390 batting average that was the highest in the major leagues in 39 years. In all, Brett would win three career batting crowns (1976, 1980, and 1990), making him the only player ever to win batting titles in three different decades. "If there was one player I ever wanted to be, it was George Brett," Milwaukee Brewers shortstop and Hall-of-Famer Robin Yount once said.

The best sidearm pitcher in baseball, Dan Quisenberry set a club record with 45 saves in **1983**.

Pitchers Dennis Leonard and Larry Gura combined to win 38 games in 1980, but Kansas City's best hurler that year—and in the decade that followed—was probably reliever Dan Quisenberry. Quisenberry had a wicked sidearm slider, and when he began throwing submarine style, he got even better. He led the AL in saves five times in the 1980s, and his lifetime ERA of 2.55 is the lowest

DAN QUISENBERRY

Like former great Frank White, shortstop Neifi Perez was known for his defense.

in Kansas City history. "I'm just a garbage man," said Quisenberry, who was always good for a quote. "I come into a game and clean up other people's mess."

Switch-hitter Willie Wilson batted over .310 and made the All-Star team in **1982** and **1983**.

Two other Kansas City standouts during the '80s were designated hitter Hal McRae and outfielder Willie Wilson. McRae was a great hitter who led the AL with 133 RBI in 1982. But perhaps his biggest contribution was his fiery leadership, and his ability to break up double plays with hard but clean slides epitomized the Royals' blue-collar style.

The switch-hitting Wilson, meanwhile, became only the second batter ever to amass 100 or more hits from both sides of the plate in a single season (1980). His speed also allowed him to cover amazing ground in the outfield and to steal bases with ease. He stole as many as 83 bases in a single season and racked up 668 total steals before

WILLIE WILSON

bringing his Kansas City career to a close. "When I get to first," Wilson explained, "I figure second and third will be mine in just a second or two."

{CROWNING THE ROYALS} Behind Brett, Quisenberry, McRae, and Wilson, Kansas City continued to win division titles in the early 1980s. In a season torn apart by a players' strike, the

Royals posted the best record in their division in the second half of the 1981 campaign, earning the right to advance to a special opening playoff round. Unfortunately, Kansas City was eliminated by the Oakland Athletics. Then, in 1984, the Royals returned to the postseason but were knocked out by the Detroit Tigers in the ALCS.

Facing such Royals pitchers as Bud Black, the Cardinals batted just .185 in the **1985** World Series.

In 1985, however, the Royals would not be denied. After edging the California Angels by one game for the division title after a dogfight that lasted until the very end of the regular season, the Royals triumphed in the ALCS. In that series, they came back from a three-games-to-one deficit to beat the Toronto Blue Jays in seven exciting contests.

In the World Series against the St. Louis Cardinals, the Royals continued to do things the hard way. As they had in the ALCS, they fell into a desperate situation, losing three of the first four games.

BUD BLACK

Hal McRae was one of the league's top designated hitters during his 14-year career.

HAL McRAE

KC

Yet amazingly, they again pulled off what seemed impossible, winning three straight games to become the first AL expansion club (team that joined the majors after 1961) to capture a world championship.

Ace Bret Saberhagen set many club records, including the most wins in a season (23 in **1989**).

Although the Royals' title run was a tremendous team effort, no one could deny the individual accomplishments of 21-year-old pitcher Bret Saberhagen, who became the youngest AL hurler ever to win the coveted Cy Young Award. Known for his great fastball and outstanding control, Saberhagen won a whopping 20 games during the 1985 season. He then earned two more victories in the World Series, including an 11–0 shutout in the deciding seventh game. "I've never seen a better young pitcher," raved St. Louis Cardinals manager Whitey Herzog. "He's phenomenal."

Saberhagen was certainly outstanding, but he wasn't the team's

BRET SABERHAGEN

only quality pitcher. In 1984 and 1985, the Royals' ace was supported by two talented lefties: Charlie Leibrandt and Bud Black, who combined for 55 wins over the course of those two seasons.

With young right-hander Mark Gubicza and the always reliable Quisenberry added to the mix, it was little wonder Kansas City rose to the top of the baseball world.

{ROUNDING OUT THE CENTURY} The Royals finished in second place a couple of times in the late 1980s but couldn't reach the World Series again. The team then slid into mediocrity despite the efforts of such players as outfielder Bo Jackson. A superb all-around athlete with unbelievable strength, Jackson had been a running back at Auburn University and won the 1985 Heisman Trophy as college football's best player. He then became a two-sport star, playing baseball in the summer and pro football in the fall.

In **1990**, Bo Jackson became the fourth Royals player ever to slam three homers in one game.

From 1987 to 1991, Jackson walloped a combined 107 homers for Kansas City, many of them traveling jaw-dropping distances. His heroics awed both fans and his fellow players before a hip injury suffered while playing football for the Oakland Raiders cut his career short. "Players from both teams watch when Bo takes batting practice," said Saberhagen. "There's always the feeling

BO JACKSON

that you're going to see something you never saw before, and we don't want to miss it."

Outfielder Tom Goodwin blazed around the bases in **1996**, stealing a total of 66 bases.

The Royals' most consistently outstanding player in the 1990s was reliever Jeff Montgomery. Statistically speaking, Montgomery was the greatest closer in team history. By the time he ended his Royals career in 1999, he had established a club record with a staggering 304 saves. Yet despite his best efforts—and those of McRae, pitcher Kevin Appier, and first baseman Wally Joyner—the Royals never seriously contended in the '90s.

In 1999, two young players gave Kansas City fans hope that the losing trend was about to end: outfielder Jermaine Dye and second baseman Carlos Beltran. Dye blasted 27 home runs that season and displayed a bazooka of an arm from right field, while the switch-hitting Beltran captured Rookie of the Year honors by

TOM GOODWIN

driving in 108 runs and showing a solid glove at second.

Two years later, Kansas City continued to build with youth by bringing in shortstop Neifi Perez. One of the game's top defensive infielders, Perez had led the National League in turning double plays from 1998 to 2000 while playing for the Colorado Rockies. The native of the Dominican Republic was also a great fastball hitter with a knack for driving the ball into the outfield alleys.

In **2000**, Jermaine Dye became the first Royals player in 11 years to win the Gold Glove award.

However, the Royals' biggest star at the turn of the 21st century was Mike Sweeney. Although he was a solid defender, the 6-foot-3 and 225-pound first baseman was best known for his powerful stroke at the plate. In 1999, the 25-year-old posted a .322 batting average. A year later, he set a new team record with 144 RBI. "He has no apparent weakness at the plate," said Oakland Athletics manager Art Howe. "He can hit the fastball, the off-speed

JERMAINE DYE

CARLOS BELTRAN

Speedy center fielder Carlos Beltran successfully stole 31 bases in 32 attempts in **2001**.

Slugging infielder Mike Sweeney provided the bulk of the Royals' offensive power.

MIKE SWEENEY

pitch, and the slider. What do you do with a guy like that?"

The Royals are justifiably proud of the seven division titles, two AL pennants, and one world championship they have captured over the course of their relatively short history. Even during the team's down years, such names as Brett, McRae, and Sweeney have given fans in Missouri reason to believe that another Royals crown is just around the corner.

Hurler Chad Durbin showed the potential to become a Royals stand-out in the 21st century.

CHAD DURBIN